I0517048

THE INVINCIBLE PRINCE
ERAY AYDIN

Translated by FATMA ERGİN DEMİR

*The prince returned with his magnificent intelligence
and incredible strategies*

to take back the thing that belongs to him!

Publisher
Cosmo Publishing

**Cosmo
Publishing
Company**

ISBN: 978-1-949872-18-7

TONGA: The blue flag empire.

KARACHI: The yellow flag empire.

SAMOA: The red flag empire.

KIRIBATI: The capital city of Tonga.

SARATOV: It is the former capital city of Tonga, which has high importance.

*****

In the times when the world was still very young, the known part of the earth was ruled by the three great states. These states were the blue-flagged TONGA representing the heavens, the red-flagged SAMOA representing the Fire, and the KARACHI Empires with the yellow flags representing the land.

TONGA was the strongest of these three states. There was AYAN, who was an excellent leader. When Ayan died in a war because of his brother's betrayal, he was left alone with his son, Caucasus. Dakar, who succeeded his brother Ayan, did not harm his nephew Caucasus. Quite the contrary, he was allowed to be a commander after having military training on the condition of his loyalty.

Caucasus, which rose to the high state of generalship at a very young age, had not lost any wars in which he fought and thus received the title of RENEWAL. The main reason for Caucasus to have won all wars was that he had the strongest intelligence ever seen. This great general managed to win all the battles with his ingenious plans.

1

In that summer, it was not only the sun that swept the earth. The three most powerful states in the world were fighting with each other.

Dakar, who was the brother of Ayan, the king of Tonga, managed to ally with Shiraz, the king of the State of Samoa, who was weak in those times. So the two states acted to occupy and divide the Karachi Empire, which was the third great power and was strengthened at that time. From now on, the balance of power would change, the number of great powers would be reduced in two, or at least we thought so.

Two armies met in Tere Desert situated in the skirts of Mount Ida. The Karachi prepared a very crowded army. A part of the desert was completely adorned by their yellow flags.

But there was the joining army of the other two empires against them. Ayan was standing in the center. The blue flag was its state flag. On the right side, there was the Shiraz army, the king of Samoa, with his proud red flag.

On the left side, there were Dakar's forces. And I, Marshal General Tomtor, was standing behind the center as a reserve force.

Ayan was so sure of the victory that he brought his eleven-year-old son, Caucasus along with him in the battlefield. Caucasus, like his father, had coy eyes and golden hair. He was the only son of Ayan, and I was responsible for his education just like with other sultan children. But beyond his warrior abilities, there were intuitive powers in him that were very important to a leader. At that moment, we were not aware of the limits of that power.

The war began with the attack of allied forces as we predicted. In the first hour, the front lines of the Karachi were cleared away. The enemy's crowded elephant herds crushed their troops immersed in their cavalry. The enemy army was showing signs of distortion in all way.

Shiraz had pushed five of the fourteen divisions under his order, so I couldn't figure out why he was so timid. On the other hand, Dakar set forth six of his eight divisions. He was also very generous and kept only the generals who were loyal to him. Ayan was very pleased with this situation. He hadn't even used his greatest forces yet. He had twenty-two divisions, except his brother and those who were with me, with twelve divisions still near him.

The result of the war seemed obvious. The Karachis' left front line was completely collapsed, and its center was under threat. Ayan looked at me over his shoulder, smiling. He said: "See? I told you. You doubted the victory for nothing,", she said. Then he did what I was scared of. He took 11 of his divisions to the battlefield. Ayan was the best commander I had ever seen, but he was always so precarious, which was his greatest weakness that would cost him the earth.

There was only one division left in the center, which was quite risky. I sent three of the five divisions with me to the center, under the command of my student, General Lima. When I started watching the war again, I noticed something terrible. The forces of Shiraz attacked our soldiers, not the Karachi. "We were betrayed!" Immediately I returned to Ayan; Ayan was left with a division in the center, and our ally Samoa army attacked Ayan with nine divisions. The three divisions I sent with Lima went not to the center, but Dakar on the left, and Dakar was watching the treacherous attack on his brother pitilessly.

I finally understood what had happened. Dakar had agreed with the Karachis and the Samoas. The aim was to kill his brother and take over the throne of Tonga empire. Who knows what he had offered the enemy in return? I was too late when I ran into the center with two divisions left.

As a result of this unexpected attack, Ayan was dead. Tonga soldiers who saw the death of their emperor began to scatter without knowing what to do. With the death of Ayan, Dakar gathered the remaining divisions and withdrew from the battlefield. Lima, my best student, also went with him. I could only save Caucasus. Together with our survivors, we retreated. The enemy did not chase us; they were busy tiring out our divisions. That day we lost almost half of our army there. And for what? To make Dakar emperor. This was the most terrible event in the history of the fight for the throne. Agreement with the enemy was the most formidable form of betrayal.

2

15 years later…

A horse red cape rider quickly entered the headquarters and galloped straight into the king's tent. When he reached the tent, the people were having a meeting inside. He entered the room without being offered, although he was covered with dust and dirt.

"What news did you bring?"

"Dear my king! The news is not good. In the south, the forces of Prince Aktobe were completely destroyed. The Prince is coming to the center with the survivor forces, and in the southwest, our army is completely defeated and unfortunately …"

"Yes, go on!"

"Sir, unfortunately, we lost the Prince, Balkas."

The king suddenly slumped down onto the seat next to him.

"Father!" It was Iber, his little son, running towards his father.

"Are you alright dad?"

The king nodded his head, yes.

"Father, please let me enter the battle and take revenge of my brother."

Falling on deaf ear, his father returned to

the messenger: "Go on! How are the other fronts?"

"Chief Lord Lima can take hold for a while, but the enemy has prepared very strong heaps, and it is constantly landing troops on land. The marshall nibs will be withdrawn today, sir!"

There were very cold air and a long silence in the headquarters. One of the commanders broke it, asking:

"Damned runner! Don't you have good news?"

Ulak answered cowardly:

"Sir, the only good news came from the Western Front where General Caucasus is. His soldiers managed to sweep the enemies down to the shore".

The commander asked suspiciously :

"Are you sure? The enemy had taken its most crowded military unit to that front after the center.

"Yes, sir, I'm sure; I saw it with my own eyes. Fiji battalions were pushed to the coastline, and some of the surviving soldiers were already leaving the peninsula. I guess there won't be one single enemy soldier left on the west side till tomorrow."

The previous moody atmosphere has given way to joy and enthusiasm now. The generals congratulated each other.

A Major General: "When the western front is cleared, the Caucasus is united with the Marshall nibs, and we can surround the enemy if we force it."

The other commanders also showed that they approved this prediction. "Halal, that boy won again! Kaz, he is the hero of Tonga!

However, this wind of joy did not seem to affect the King. When the soldiers in the tent noticed it, they kept quiet. Even they were ashamed of what they did. After all, the king had just lost his son.

After a short silence, the king ordered the intelligence officer: "Tell my nephew to leave the western front and come to the center!".

The soldiers looked at each other baffled and confused. "But, sir ..." The king raised his hand and gestured to shut up.

"Don't argue with me; just do what I say. We're shrinking the front to fight from a single center".

We were all surprised when the withdrawal order came to the headquarters. The Caucasus welcomed it calmly: "What are they trying to do, those idiots? They took half of the divisions in our hands. We're about to win a victory, and they tell us to step back".

"As you taught me, Master Tomtom; orders are never questioned."

"But not such a dick!" Caucasus smiled.

"I have nothing to do, master! My uncle has a know".

Dakar, with my persistence, did nothing to Caucasus and allowed him to live. He also did not take his dignity rights. After Dakar became the emperor, he announced my student Lima the Commander-in-Chief and the Speaker. And I was an ordinary general.

I didn't tell Caucasus about his uncle's betrayal, it would have made everything worse, but I raised him with my own hands, I taught him everything I knew, to the finest detail. He became a general at the age of fourteen, and since then, he had achieved a hundred and eighty-six victories in the last twelve years. No defeat. They called him "Invincible" because there was no other general who had never sustained a defeat on Earth and had won so many battles in such a short time. His reputation was so great that the great commanders who wanted to go down in history as the first person to beat him risked their careers, but they all failed in the end.

Our current enemies were Fiji Khanate. The Fiji were sailors that descended from the Samoa and were under the command of the Samoa. Since the place we fought for was a peninsula, we saw the Fiji as the enemy, but behind the scenes, there was the Kingdom of Samoa.

The commander-in-chief of Samoa took over the forces that attacked the western front instead of the central forces. Although it was three times more in amount, the center was constantly recruiting soldiers of ours with various excuses. The king and some of his men wanted us to be defeated. Finally, we had eleven divisions against the seven divisions of the enemy. However, Caucasus again made his speech. In spite of all our oppositions, he allowed the enemy to the land with all his forces. He then placed six of the eleven divisions in an area between the two peaks, which was the narrowest point of the enemy's passageway, placing the remaining five divisions behind them. Thus, we were able to feed the forefront with the divisions of the rear, and we could always bring out fresh and never decreasing forces against the enemy. On top of the hills on both sides, Caucasus set up two archer regiments, which he specially raised. The enemy who lost their ships could no longer be fed from the rear with a night raid. Despite all their efforts, they began to disintegrate. The place we fought was rock, and there was little greenery, and the rest were stony. Thousands of people died for this steep rock with no plants grown. The forces of the two sides were balanced within a week. It seems Caucasus was winning again until this annoying news came.

"What are we going to do?"

"So are we going to lose when we're about to win? Don't you get it? Your uncle is willing to lose a war to end your name".

"What do you suggest?

"Let's pretend we didn't know; we'll win the war tomorrow, let's just pretend it's a day late."

"My uncle won't buy it."

"Be it so or not, he can not punish a victorious commander for this."

After standing up and stretching out from where he was, Caucasus took a tour inside the room. He was incredibly calm. I could never understand his calmness. After his father's death, he turned out to be extremely self-confident and careless.

"No, master! The traditions of Tonga are more important than my triumph if we do what you say in the future, the soldiers will try not to listen and do their own business. This would weaken the military discipline."

"So, what are we going to do? Will we go away leaving everything behind?"

"Yes, of course!". Afterwards, he called the commander: "Get ready, we are leaving."

3

By leaving a war that we were about to win, we started to retreat towards the cliffs like cowards. I was no longer familiar with such things; the disgust of politics was nothing. It wasn't the first time I had seen that external interests were ignored for internal balances.

Tonga army was drawn towards the mountains. Preparing to return to its country, the Fiji people stopped picking up their luggage and started to chase us. Luckily, we had done the escape properly. It took them a long time to realize that we went away as they did not expect it. But when they realized, they began to chase us with a gleaming enthusiasm.

We were a day away from the headquarters while the enemy was a few hours away. It was only a matter of time before they got to us. That is when the mistake of the decision was better understood. With the withdrawal, we not only dropped the western wing but also caused the enemy's central winding. I hated the king once again because of this historical error, when would this man learn to value his country? But he wasn't the only one I was angry with. I was angry with Caucasus, who was bound to his father's murderous uncle with an eternity of faith and did all he said. He also undermined his country's interests.

We came to the exit of a narrow canyon that Caucasus stopped the army and ordered it to take a war position.

"What are you trying to do?"

"I got a plan, master!"

"Are we going to fight?"

"Yes."

"But this place is not suitable to fight at all; ten soldiers side by side can even hardly walk."

Caucasus by spreading his confident smile on his face again: "Don't worry, Master, it's not a problem we have to think about," he said. There were voices on both sides of the canyon. When I looked up, I saw that archer regiments of the Caucasus settled on the right and left sides of the canyon. None of the commanders there noticed when he planned and how he did all these things.

After leaving a battalion with a lance on the exit of the canyon, the rest of us were drawn back, and we were waiting with our weapons. I understood Caucasus's plan, but the archers were very close to the exit. Instead of attacking, the enemy could retreat and try to move over the galleon, leaving us in a very difficult position. However, I did not mention it to the commander because if I knew Caucasus, he must have thought about it before. A little later, the enemy entered the canyon; the red flags and guns were noticed. Yes, they noticed us and immediately embraced their weapons. First of all, he had some proud commanders. He was extremely arrogant as he thought that we escaped because we were so scared of him. He poured out orders to his men. He probably thought we were getting ready for war because we couldn't escape.

A few minutes later, the riders attacked us with their infantry at the back. They were galloping on us and were unaware of the surprise they would encounter soon. Interestingly, what I thought at the time was not the attack of the enemy to us, but it was the sound of water I heard. The nearest river was about two hours away, but the sound was very clearly heard, which meant that the rain caused the river to overflow. That sound was soothing for me. I looked at Caucasus standing right next to me, and he also seemed comfortable. Maybe he was influenced by the sound of water too.

The enemy was halfway through the canyon; a terrible noise was heard deafening one's ears. From above, the rocks began to fall on both sides of the canyon, and on the army of the enemy which snaked along the canyon. The rocks destroyed the divisions at the back of the enemy. At least five divisions died under the rocks. The rest first paused and looked at the hills, and then at their dying friends. They were very angry; they started to come towards us with a great temper. But there was the same noise again. This time the giant rocks had fallen to the forefront of the battalion, and thousands were dead again, and the survivors were stuck in the canyon.

The enemy army was squeezed between two rocky cliffs, and only a few battalions outside the rock were commanders and soldiers. Their back was closed, and in front of them, it was the big Tonga army. We couldn't make sense of what happened, and we were just as surprised as our enemies. What was that noise, and how did the rocks break? Even at that moment, I interpreted it as a gift from God. When we were confused, looking confused, that same noise was heard again. The river also started to run from the sky down to the rocks over the enemy army. The enemy tried not to drown in the canyon as they were struggling to overcome the cliffs. At that time, the archers began to throw arrows without cease upon the soldiers trying to escape while they let others drown.

The commander, who understood that he had lost his army, had two options; either he would commit suicide with his soldiers left or he would surrender. He chose the latter.

4

"No news from my nephew?"

"Not yet, dear, my king."

"I wonder why there is no answer. It has been four days since we sent the message.

There was no answer. His supervisor bowed his head forward two hands tied forward. The king continued rubbing his beard. Like he was talking to himself.

"He did not listen to me as he was his own man, which I was expecting." His nephew was very loyal to him, but the king still expected him to betray him one day. He was often provoking Caucasus and giving a chance to him to do so. But Caucasus was as loyal as his sons. This made the king very angry.

"Your Majesty,it is a matter of urgency!" The messenger intruding inside got the king out of his deep dream world. The king ordered the adviser to walk away, pointing with his hand. After the consultant went out, the messenger began to talk.

"Sir, the forces of General Caucasus came, and they destroyed the forces of Fiji in the west!"

"What! Didn't I tell them to come back with no war? How do they dare to oppose my order!"

"Sir, I have no idea, but there is the commander of the Fiji army with them in the west as a prisoner".

"Call Caucasus immediately here".

"Err, sir...".

Didn't you hear me canine, call my nephew!".

"Sir, Caucasus is not at the head of the army!"

"What do you mean by saying 'not at the head'?"

"Sir, the commander Caucasus, General Tomtor, and a few battalions left the army and went somewhere else."

"Where did they go?"

The messenger turned as red as a beetroot.

"Well, sir, nobody knows about it"

"Call immediately the commanders of the soldiers who came to me."

"Yes sir!" the messenger flew out.

5

We were leaving the army with a group of soldiers in a different direction, but the only person who knew where we were going was Caucasus. I did not ask him because I was so sure that he would never tell it. After a period galloping at the point where the valley became steep, we slowed down; with our horses side by side.

Will you talk?

"Talk what?"

"About what happened in the canyon. I wondered how those rocks broke off and fell over the Fijis. Besides, how did you manage to change the bed of that big river in a very short time?

Caucasus took his hand to his waist and took out a velvet pouch. "With this," he gave me the pouch. It looked like a cash pouch, but there was no money in it.

"What is this?" I said and opened the pouch. There was black powder inside. "They say it is gunpowder."

"Magical black powder! Oh my God! Where did you get it from?"

"It wasn't me. The secret men found it". The secret men were the name of the intelligence agency of Caucasus. I didn't even know the people in this organization, but in it, they would only obey Caucasus, neither the king knew him, nor Marshall. The only leader for them is Caucasus! These people had a huge contribution to the incredible success of Caucasus. He chose these people from among the wretched people he had donated their lives, and raised them and gave them important duties. So these men and women had a deep commitment to him and were willing to dare to die for him. Caucasus thus became aware of everything that had

14

happened in the world, in the country or all the palaces, and was never blindsided. Caucasus continued his speech.

"I sent my spies all around the world because I wanted to be aware of each scientific development. My men reaching everywhere found and brought me several war guns. One of the most important war guns was the formula of gun powder."

"What? You mean you know the formula of gun powder?"

"Shhh! Slow down. I don't want anybody to hear."

"Now, I see how you managed to break off and change the river bed. Of course, this also explains the horrific rumble."

"It does."

"You know what? You can take over my uncle".

He raised his well-known laughter again. "Master, I told you before, I don't have my eyes on my uncle's throne."

"But why? I have difficulty understanding you, my son. Once you revolt against him, all officers will back you. You know this."

He pointed out at me with his finger to pause and then dismounted from his horse quickly. We did the same thing. By taking out our guns, we silently marched on towards the rocks. When I lifted my head and looked around from the rocks, I couldn't believe my eyes. There was the headquarters of the Fiji in front of me. It was a valley surrounded by the steep rocks. Now we understand why we could not find this place till now because when looked from outside, the valley was not showing up. There were 15 division soldiers in the valley. Besides, their masters and Samoas' messengers were walking around. They seemed to be preparing for dinner. While our enemies' cookers were boiling, the soldiers were taking out their plates. At this moment, some men went out of the tent, at the backside of the valley, which was bigger and more decorated than the others and where there were guardians at the door. I recognized one of them. It was the Prince of Fiji.

"So this was your plan."

"Yes, we will kidnap the prince with a raid."

"If we attack the whole army, wouldn't it be easier?"

"No, if we are crowded, the raid will lose its quality. This is their home. No matter how many people we are, they will destroy us in this valley".

He was right as usual. I was not going to ask how he found this place because I knew more than anybody else about what his intelligence could do. The best thing we had to do was to kidnap the prince with a raid, and I was sure that Caucasus also had a plan for it.

6

Secret Men or the Caucasus' mysterious soldiers approached very secretly and neutralized the guards at the top. But this was not enough.

"What will happen to other guards? We have to kill the other guards at the entrance of the valley. Otherwise, the raid will fail."

"Don't worry master; we're not going to do the raid."

"What do you mean?"

At that moment a shepherd appeared behind the mountains. He had hundreds of sheep. However, those sheep were carrying small panniers tied on their backs.

"What is this?"

Caucasus pointed at the shepherd with his head. The shepherd also nodded as if he approved something. Then he started to pipe. There was a big ram on the front. The ram slowly started to walk towards the valley of the Fijis. The herd was following it. By the way, The Secret Men were burning the wicks on the sheep.

"Are those gunpowder in the pannier?"

Caucasus laughed but did not say anything. In the end, the shepherd started to pipe faster, and then the ram at the forefront started to run towards the headquarters with hundreds of sheep behind.

The Fijis, who watched the sheep with surprise, accepted this as a blessing of the God of ram they worshiped and opened the doors of the entrance. The guards did not oppose. Yes indeed, the Fiji people worshiped the ram and the goat. I respect people's religious beliefs. However, if you worship and eat the sheep... You're not that very smart person. Anyway, they were the Fijis who welcomed the hundreds of sheep coming. It was too late when they noticed the panniers and the burning wick on the sheep they caught. The sheep spreading all over the headquarters began to explode one after the other. Every single sheep was destroying tens of Fijis. But it was the panic and defeat atmosphere of the explosions. No matter how crowded and powerful an army is, it begins panic in the army. Especially if they feel like their gods do not protect them, that army would probably be defeated.

Caucasus jumped on his horse and took out his sword.

"My lions! Let's hunt some rams," he shouted.

We launched into the Fiji headquarters.

We already defeated the Fijis and already captured the prince within a very short time.

7

It was worth seeing our king's face when he saw that his nephew, whom he had been waiting for to scold or even punish, had returned with the enemy commander. When we talked about what happened, the whole command echelon had listened to us with admiration and without a word. They all looked at us with great admiration, except for our great king, he didn't seem very pleased with what happened, but he couldn't say it among everybody. He just kept up with a simple greeting and gave him another medal of bravery. Now we won the war, and although all the commanders, including Lima, who passed through my place, were defeated, it was the victory of our army. Now it was time to celebrate.

We went back to the capital. Our capital's name was: Kiribati.

Kiribati was a lush and rainy city, where small rivers flow through and where red roofs covered the small concrete houses widespread. The modern city and nature were intertwined here. On one side there were wide and long paths consisting of symmetrical stone blocks; on the other side, grapevines were reaching out from the houses' balconies to the gardens like a tulle of a bride.

In this place where sardines were surrounded by carnations and where surrounds all paths like a warden, the traditional clothes of the girls were the floral motifs on their white dresses and the daisies they made crowns for their hair. The girls of this beautiful city, which was created by scraping into a forest, were the most beautiful ornaments of the city with those white dresses that wrapped their bronze skin and the flowers adorning their bodies.

All the houses in our capital were similar to those of brothers from the same parents. The houses with two storeys in general, sometimes with three or four storeys were adorned by grapevines and colorful flowers like the flowers of the girls in their white dresses, who were living in these houses. Our houses with big and comfortable rooms and sunken balconies whose sequential columns were aligned across the façade, seemed as if they were not human-made but a part of nature when looked from the top although it might look a bit smaller from the outside.

State buildings, which are larger than individual houses, were generally located at the intersection of roads and they are near the road with small lakes. The city walls surrounding the whole city like a diamond necklace were a sign of the beauty of the city, fascinated by the power of the city. Because of these walls, there were army headquarters in front of the two existing exit doors, and this army was the most powerful on the earth. So this beautiful girl's angry and mighty brother was waiting to scratch eyes out of the ones who were looking crossed eye at her, with a fist without sleeping day and night.

Tonga's guards were met with flowers and celebrations by the people they died for that day. Our arrival in the city was splendid. When we entered the city from the big street leading to the palace, there was a festive atmosphere in the country, jugglers were jumping up, and the streets equipped with flags and flowers were full of people. Children and young girls were throwing roses and tulips on our heads.

In spite of all the censorship, the people were celebrating Prince Caucasus, who had received even more attention than the king. We were able to cross the famous Saltanat Street that went to the palace in almost an hour, though the celebrations continued as we reached the palace. The worst part of the victory was celebrations after the victory. No one remembers the ones who died there. Everybody has fought, but only survivors are rewarded; which is ridiculous for me. It has always been harder for me to show up than to fight against the enemy with a sword.

Our palace was located at the highest point of the city and was in a controlling position. When we geographically accepted the city walls as the borders of the city, it was almost in the middle of the city. The three-storey royal house was made of pure gold bricks, with marble blocks and silver brackets added. The window sills and balcony ornaments were adorned with various precious rocks, especially ruby and sapphire. The great fun lasted until the morning of the next day and tired my old body as much as the battle.

We learned the death of Balkash just before dinner, and we were all put off. Balkash was my favorite among the princes; Caucasian loved him too among all his cousins. Balkash was not as stupid as his brother Aktobe nor fearful as his brother, Iber. He was a good patriotic commander. Alas, death took him early.

Nobody spoke for a long time at dinner. The royal family and the senior civil and military bureaucrats attended the dinner. Aktobe was the elder brother who broke the silence and started to talk.

"Dear father and dear guests! I would like to give you one more good news on this beautiful day that we see the victory of our armies: Mercan and I have decided to get married."

Everybody was taken aback. Mercan was brought to Kiribati as a slave when she was a child, but thanks to her incredible beauty, she turned out to be a respected woman in the palace instead of being a ordinary odalisque.

Mercan was seven years younger than Aktobe and six years than Caucasus. Mercan has always been with Caucasus for many years, and even they were engaged until two years ago. However, after a fight between them, they broke down and did not come together again. Nobody knew what they talked or what caused them to leave. But they both still loved each other. There was no evidence to prove it, but I could feel it.

Caucasus was influenced by the news as much as we were. His face color turned white. I've never seen him like this even during the hardest times in the battlefield. I felt the need to intervene.

"Aktobe, when your brother was just martyred, a marriage becomes disrespectful to the memory of your brother."

"Master, I have never said I was getting married now. I just gave you a piece of good news to break up the gloomy atmosphere of my brother's death knell. Didn't you like the news?"

The king intervened. "We all liked the news. Let's organize the wedding ceremony right after the funeral." After that, everybody started to applaud and congratulate them.

While the dinner was about to end, our majesty raised his hand and paused everyone to start to talk addressing to Caucasus:

"My successful general, I am thinking about giving you another mission".

Caucasus was serious: "It is my command."

"If you feel tired, it can wait."

"There is no need sir. I am listening to you".

"Good. You know Burke, don't you?"

"Of course, he is one of our best generals.

He supported me a lot".

"I want you to kill him!"

"What!"

I couldn't stop yelling while Caucasus stayed calm.

"He revolted a couple of weeks ago and captured Tasahuz Fort with his soldiers. He was supported by the public too. As you know, it is hard to capture that fort. If someone can do it, it is only you. But first, try to persuade him because he is a very serviceable general. If he appeals for mercy, I forgive him. Kill him if he does not give up the riot. By the way, try to rescue the castellan he took as a slave; of course, if he is still alive."

8

While Mercan was wandering through the palace garden, she was startled when she met Caucasus.

"Ahh, it was you!"

Caucasus brought a flower and gave it to her.

"Were you expecting someone else?" he smiled. "Or your beloved fiancee, Aktobe?"

Mercan was ashamed. Although they were separate, they belonged to each other. She felt like she was betraying her lover.

"I swear I did not know. Aktobe told me that he wanted to marry me. I severely refused him. He presented with a fait accompli in the evening. What will we do now?"

"I have nothing to do. I wish you happiness. Give your first child my name, and that is all." Mercan got angry a lot: "Pig! I will marry that stupid Aktobe just to spite."

As she turned away, Caucasus took her and turned to himself and kissed her for long. When their lips parted, she watched Caucasus with her beautiful black eyes for a while. Then she gave him a hard slap.

"Don't do this again!"

Caucasus laughed: "You used to love it before."

"It was before. Before you cheated on me."

"I never cheated on you."

"But you will. And you will use me!"

"Ok, leave it at that. Or someone will hear us and misunderstand."

They both paused and watched each other for a while. Then Mercan broke the silence.

"I used to love your father, Ayan, a lot, like my own father. He rescued me and raised me like his daughter."

"I know."

"Do you remember what he told us before he went to his last travel?"

"Yes, I do. He told me that you were going to be my wife or my sister. Als, he said that we should decide on it."

"Well, what have you become? You've become neither my sister nor my lover!"

"We are in love with each other."

"But we will never belong to each other!"

"Isn't there something to do to have you back?"

"There is, Caucasus, but I am sure you won't do it."

Mercan left the garden, smelling the flower in her hand.

9

As Caucasus never objected to his uncle, we went on the road the next day of the victory. We have taken a couple of divisional troops with us, but we could only repress this rebellion with the entire army of Tonga. Burke was a soldier I knew very well, and I saw his talents. He was also a prominent general. Tasauz was a fortress impossible to invade; a place where the mountain carved inside was so high and steep to reach the ones from inside. Although it was close to the enemy's border, it had never been invaded until now. The only way to get to this fortress was a footpath carved into the edge of the cliff. You couldn't pass on a horse.

We have arrived at the skirts of Tasau mountain where the fortress was carved inside. But there was a huge mountain in front of us. If the flag of Tonga waving at the top of the mountain did not exist, nobody could imagine that there was a fortress here. I never doubted that the archers, who were surely placed all over the mountain, would hunt us one by one while we were on the path.

"Are you aware that we can not capture this place?"

"Of course, I know."

"Then what will we do?"

He got off his horse. "I will go there alone."

"Are you crazy?"

"Burke will like me."

"Yes, but it does not mean that he won't kill you."

"You are very dubious, master."

"That is why I am alive. You shouldn't go there alone, Caucasus."

Surely he did not listen to me. He is his father's son. By leaving his guns, he started to proceed on the path. They aimed crossbows at him.

Just after Caucasus faded away, a group of soldiers in yellow uniforms cut him off. They were the guards of the palace who supported the revolt.

"What are you doing here your royal highness?"

"I need to talk to General Burke." After looking at each other in hesitation for a minute:

They said, "Welcome your royal highness!"

and took him to their impossible to enter-place.

The gigantic gates of the Tasauz fortress were opened. Those who saw the entrants stopped their work and started to whisper and gather together. Caucasus walking with three guards was brought in front of a large white tent. Next to the tent, there was a throne made of wood and adorned with cushions. The guard in front ran into the tent. After a short while, he and a strong, hefty, tall man with a thick mustache and a sword, in leather clothes, came out. He had a vintage soldier stance.

"Welcome Prince Caucasus."

"Thanks, General Burke."

General sat back on his throne. "To what do I owe your visit, your majesty?"

"I have come here to dissuade you from the revolt and take back the castellan by command of the King Dakar."

Burke burst into laughter. "The king? Is he the king? He is one of the most coward and vulgar men I have ever seen in my life. He's a bastard who sold his brother to the enemy. Yes, you know that too. Though nobody talked about it, we all know, including you. that bastard Dakar got our majesty Ayan killed."

Caucasus continued as if he did not hear anything.

"The king Dakar promised you to restore your old mission and title if you forgo the riot."

"He promised. Huh! How can I trust such an unvirtuous person's words?"

"I do guarantee you on it. Don't you trust me too?"

"I would die for you!"

"So the king…"

Burke stood up. "God damn the king! The only king for me was General Ayan. I only devoted myself to him".

"My father died many years ago, Burke!".

"Yes, your vulgar uncle killed him."

"It is not for a soldier to intervene with politics. Let the riot end, please."

"Damn you! We have supported you. Why did not you overthrow your uncle when you had a chance?" When Caucasus began to win their first victory, almost all the commanders came together, and we had a secret meeting. At the meeting, we asked Caucasus to take down Dakar and succeed him, but Caucasus opposed to this extremely simple revolution and said that he did not intend to be king. Dakar was a very untalented king, and he was not a good person. He was always making wrong decisions, displacing people unjustly or raising those who didn't deserve. In our country, injustice, nepotism and bribery were not as increased as in his period. Caucasus won the love and respect of the people, the army and the bureaucrat. People missed the days with Ayan. Caucasus was so incomparably good like his father. That was why many commanders, especially Burke and I, asked him to take the lead. If he had wanted, we could have done it in a couple of hours, but Caucasus refused it every time.

"I told you before; I am a soldier. I can't rule the state."

"Come on! You are the greatest leader throughout human history. Tell me why? Why do you obey and protect your vulgar uncle? Why don't you take him down?"

"Enough! I am not here to talk about politics. Just end the riot and turn the castellan over to me!"

Burke pointed at a child with his finger. When Caucasus looked at the child, he saw that he lacked one arm. "Do you know what happened to the child's arm?"

"No."

"He, who you risked your life to rescue, wanted to have the mother of this boy. When the woman resisted, he cut the child's arm in front of his mother. She had to sacrifice herself to save her child. Is that your castellan? There are plenty of such assholes among rulers all over the country. And your king, who you don't allow anyone to speak ill of him, brought them to power."

"I am so sorry! But you can not judge him. The only one who will judge him is the justice of Tonga. Please stop the riot!"

Burke smiled: "What if I refuse it?"

"Then I will have to kill you."

Burke laughed again. "Slow down, young prince. You can be inconvincible but how can you prevent me from killing you here as you are alone?"

At that moment, two guards in yellow uniforms, standing at Burke's right and left side, turned their crossbows into Burke. One of them had brought Caucasus. Like everyone else, Burke was very surprised. After a while, he started to laugh out loud.

"You placed spy here, huh?"

"Yes."

"How could you do that?"

"I can place a spy wherever I want."

"Wow! You were smarter than I thought."

"Thanks."

"But you are mistaken at one point."

"About what?"

"You can't stop me like this."

"You mean we are going to fight?"

Burke took out his sword. Caucasus pointed at the guards to put their guns down. Burke jumped down from the throne at one swoop.

One of the soldiers gave Caucasus a sword.

General, who said, "Your Majesty, I give my respects to you," prostrated before Caucasus, which was a ritual when someone challenges a royal person.

"Please Burke. You don't need to do it".

"Draw your sword, my majesty!"

"Burke, please don't!" Caucasus had an appealing voice because he never wanted to hurt such a precious and kindhearted commander.

"Please draw your sword, my majesty!"

"No."

"I have to kill you then. I can't serve for that damn man". Burke ran to Caucasus swinging up his sword. He was crying. The moment when Caucasus pulled his sword and sank it in Burke's chest at a speed that no one could understand while Burke was drawing his sword.

Burke's sword fell first, and then he collapsed. He was smiling.

"I've always wanted such an honorable death."

"Sleep in peace, master."

Burke squinted his eyes on a smiley face. Then he fell to the ground and closed his eyes forever.

Caucasus gave an order: "Bring the castellan immediately!"

They did. Soon after, the castellan appeared. He seemed like a self-seeking merchant with a long dress rather than a soldier with his skinny body, pointed nose, and bald head on top. The castellan was running towards Caucasus by hanging the flags out. He bent down to the ground.

"Welcome, your majesty. You just arrived on time. Otherwise, they would kill me." When he saw the dead body of Burke, he spat on it. "You have bumped off bastard Burke. Don't worry; I will get others killed. Will you go now or stay for the night?" Caucasus ignored that sucker and disgusting man. Again he became incredibly cold-blooded.

"No. I have to go right now!".

"Uh! I am sorry about it. Don't worry; I will report the king about how you saved my life alone."

Caucasus had a sad face. "It was not as you exaggerated."

"Noo! You just arrived on time."

"It wasn't…"

"What do you mean?"

"Unfortunately I wasn't on time. You were already killed when I arrived.".

The castellan turned pale. "What?... What did you say?"

Caucasus leaned over and took Burke's knife from his belt and stabbed the castellan's heart without saying anything. The castellan's face was horrible as if he were trying to figure out what was going on. His eyes were wide open.

After the fall of the castellan, Caucasus returned to the people who were shocked and said: "Go to your houses, you are free. Nobody will hurt you" and looked at Burke: "Don't worry, Master, no one can harm your people, I promise you!"

10

It was very quiet after the end of the riot for two months. We sat in our houses and enjoyed the capital.

Thanks to the policies of our king (!), as we were the enemies of great powers, it was the longest time in the last three years with no war. This holiday was very good, especially for me. I could spend a lot of time with my family because I couldn't see their faces for a long time. Caucasus also rested a lot. I haven't seen him have such a good time. But one evening, when one of the royal messengers came to my house and told me to come to the palace for a very urgent meeting, I realized that this beautiful holiday was over.

When I got to the palace's meeting room, I saw that I was the last to come. All force commanders, experts, senior diplomats, and bureaucrats arrived there. Marshal Lima was also there. At the entrance, we caught our eyes for a while. What a shameless man he was! He betrayed me and the ex-sultan but still, he could look into my eyes with a smirking face.

After entering, I sat next to Caucasus by saluting the king and the delegation. There was a tense atmosphere; I soon understood why. Our ancient enemies, the Samoa and the Karachi, had made an alliance against us. We had the intelligence on good authority, namely on Caucasus; so no one questioned the news.

The following is a summary of the information: Since Karachi Emperor Herat died last summer, his daughter Rat succeeded him. This was within our knowledge, but we did not know that the new and very young queen had formed an alliance with the king of Samoa, Shiraz and agreed to destroy us. Even according to information, one of their

33

armies had already set out to occupy Keta Fortress. At the end of the discussions, it was decided that a commander would go to Keta Fortress to protect the castle. There were discussions about who would be. General Marshall Lima had once again thought something wicked:

"I think we should send our best commander to the fortress."

All eyes were on Caucasus. It doesn't take a genius to understand Lima's treacherous plans. Apparently, Lima was trying to finish Caucasus. Of course, I opposed to it, but no one else dared to oppose to Marshall. Moreover, there was a point at which he was right: Keta was our weak point in the south, and if it fell, the road to the capital would be defenseless. The decision was finally made. Caucasus would go to Keta with five divisions. They also gave me the duty of gathering cavalry troops not to send me with him.

Caucasus, on the other hand, set out with his usual oppressed attitude without any objection; on the other hand, Marshall made his first treachery and gave him only one division and said that he would send the rest next week. Caucasus did not object to it either.

When he arrived at Keta, the situation did not look too bright. The enemy was one day away and very well prepared. They were a crowded army and with an experienced commander from Samoa, General Dese. The situation of the fortress was not very pleasant. Its position was very unfavorable to defend. It was in a plain terrain except for the wood-hills behind. Since he had not seen any danger for a long time, he did not have enough heaps or military. After the condition assessment with the fortress staff, he announced his decision:

"We are evacuating the fortress."

There were oppositions. "No sir, we can not leave the fortress. It is extremely a vantage point."

"I know, but we will evacuate anyway."

The castellan couldn't wait. "Sir, you are recognized by your courage, and do you mean we should escape? I know the hard situation we are in, but it is not a reason to escape like those cowards. If you want, you can leave, but I can not accept it. My friends and I will stay and fight."

Caucasus listened to the castellan quietly and stood to say: "Tonight we will completely evacuate the fortress till midnight. Inside, I will only have the barrels that I brought and my team of ten people. Everybody else, including the commands, will take all movables and go back to the hills behind the fortress." The castellan resented a bit. Once he was about to say something, Caucasus left away.

Caucasus had brought the archer regiments with him. After placing his troops in the hills, the soldiers started to wait in the wood. The enemy could come at any time.

When it was nearly an hour, the enemy's red bricks began to be seen on the horizon. The castellan was eating his heart out because the fortress had become his home for years. He gave his twenty years to this cairn. He felt like as if he had to leave his lover to another man. He looked daggers at Caucasus. He hates him to death. He reveals it with his looks. By the way, the enemy arrived in front of the fortress, which is in an abandoned condition with its doors open. The useless goods were lying in front of the castle. The paper and cloth pieces lifted by the wind were swinging from one side to another on the desert soil.

When the enemy realized that the fortress had been abandoned, there was laughter among the army. The laughter and ridicule of the soldiers were heard by the

Tongas. The castellan was willing to die a thousand times instead of hearing them. It was impossible now. Within a few minutes, two-thirds of the army had already entered the fortress. It was theirs now. I wish I hadn't seen this image. Instead, I wish I had seen the fortress disappear. The moment the castellan finished his call, the fortress blew up with a deafening noise.

Keta Castle was destroyed by the intruders inside. The explosion was so severe that even a small number of soldiers left outside were killed or injured. Even General Dese was among those injured. Meanwhile, the castellan watching the state of the fortress felt piggy in the middle. He looked at Caucasus as though seeking an answer but he was interested in something else. He was looking at up to ten soldiers from the woods. They immediately stood against Caucasus.

"Sir, the mission is completed successfully."

"Injury?"

"No sir, we are all fine."

"Congratulations, kids. You did a great job".

Soldiers said all together: "Thank you, sir."

When the vast majority of the enemy army disappeared, the archers and other archers of Caucasus started hunting the rest. Caucasus ordered all his soldiers to attack a few scared and shocked soldiers so that the army could feel the victory. Right after his order, the soldiers, who thought that they would hide like cowards, suddenly flowed into the battlefield. It didn't take long for them to destroy the enemy army.

The enemy army had been destroyed except a few dozen prisoners. There was General Dese among the prisoners. Caucasus looked after Dese, treating him with his wounds privately in his tent, and then released him. Nobody could make sense of it, but no one asked why, because Caucasus was never asked why. He must have known something.

The castellan, who had been wandering in the ruined fortress, was pleased with the result, but when he saw Caucasus, he walked toward him: "Sir, I apologize you. I dared to sail into your courage and intelligence. So I deserve punishment from you".

Caucasus smiled. He put his hand on the castellan's shoulder: "You are not that wrong. Your fortress has gone."

"Don't worry, sir." Showing the trophies of the enemy left on the ground, he said: "We could build a much stronger fortress than before."

11

After returning to Kiribati, Caucasus became more famous, but he seemed unhappy somehow. In the next morning of his arrival, he went to "Hidden Heaven", a garden with a large pool, where there were thousands of flowers and plants behind the palace. It wasn't prohibited for the courtiers to enter "Hidden Heaven," but the king and the women in the palace usually used to go there, which was a kind of tradition. It had been the first time since his childhood that Caucasus went down to this garden on that morning right after breakfast.

Dozens of girls and women of the palace were walking along with the pool, laughing and talking. When they saw Caucasus, they were a little surprised, and they stopped talking, but it did not last. After all, he was a gentleman; they had already seen him in other parts of the palace. Only the young girls who liked Caucasus talked and continued to laugh at each other, but Caucasus was interested in someone else. He was gazing at a beautiful brunette girl with black hair and black eyes, sitting alone in the corner by the girls. The girl got up and entered the deserted rose garden on the other side of the big pool. Caucasus followed her too.

When Caucasus went to her side, they both looked at each other for a while. The girl broke the silence first.

"What do you want, Caucasus? Or do you want a new slap on your face?".

Caucasus smiled and then became serious again.

"I want you to come back to me, Mercan."

"That is impossible."

"Why?"

"You know why."

"If it is because of the things between us, I am so sorry."

"There is no point in talking about these things. I am engaged."

"This engagement has no value. You are not in love with him!"

"You are not in love with me, either."

"How do you know that?"

"You are not because you wanted to use me for your bloody desires."

"It is not true!"

"How did you forget the thing you asked me for?"

When Caucasus remembered why they argued, he had a sad face.

"It was a mistake. I shouldn't have asked you such a thing."

"Yeah, you shouldn't!"

After a short silence, Mercan continued:

"Did you give up what you planned?"

"No."

"Well, if I told you I would come back to you, would you give up?"

Caucasus said in a very decisive tone: "No!".

"There, your love is. It is nothing. I don't want to see you anymore. Besides, I will pray every day for your failure!" she walked away without a backward glance. Caucasus did nothing but desperately watched her go away. He remembered such desperation the last time when his father was killed in front of him.

Caucasus told Mercan his most crucial secret and asked her for help. It was obvious how much he loved her. Mercan did never betray him or his love either although she refused Caucasus' request, which I had no idea about in those times. She always kept his secret despite their fights.

In the evening, Caucasus and Mercan met again. Caucasus was watching Mercan without any shyness while Mercan deliberately came close to her fiancee. The entertainment was kept short because the country was still under thread.

After the entertainment, the divan of the rulers in the state gathered again, but this time, I was not late for the meeting. First, the meeting began with the celebration in the name of Caucasus, then the main issue was discussed. The Karachi and the Samoa people had prepared a big army of alliances and set out for us. However, our forces did not yet reach the desired level. Although I had managed to collect a large part of the cavalry, the army still lacked many things. So we needed at least ten days to prepare us for the defense.

After the new vehement and long-lasting discussions, the most difficult work in this country, as there was no other commander, was Caucasus' as usual. My opposition, of course, did not work because Caucasus had approved the mission without any objections. The mission was: Caucasus would take fifteen divisions or so and go to our headquarters in Samara Valley. He would stall the enemy as long as he could, and we would complete the necessary preparations. If he could keep the enemy for more than fifteen days, he would come back with the remaining soldiers.

It was a simple but logical plan. It was the only thing that could be done in such a situation. We had to gain time. Besides, Caucasus was the only person to achieve the impossible. This time I was going with him and I did not intend to appease about this issue, and nobody objected me to go with him.

12

When we arrived in Samara, we saw five divisions, many of which were infantry divisions. We brought fifteen divisions with us. We had twenty divisions and a few regiments in total.

After the situation assessment with local commanders, we understood that the danger was greater than we thought. According to the intelligence reports, there were sixty-three alliance forces, which meant our triple. This was, in fact, a soluble problem. The scariest thing for us was the great number of their elephants: over five hundred, which was the greatest number I have ever seen.

Together with Caucasus, we visited the place where the war would take place, and we made our investigations. The war would be on a wide plain. This was a vast plain that looked like an infertile desert just before the Samara Valley. There was a narrow road connecting the Samara Valley with this vast plain, which was formed by carving the mountain. We would take this mountain and the alley behind us as suitable with the traditional war strategy of Caucasus. The mountain was a great chance for us because we were going to fight for defense rather than have a battle due to our lack of power.

"What will happen to the elephants Caucasus?"

"I haven't got any idea yet."

"But we need to do something."

"I know, but what? We don't have any strategy to stop them."

"We might deploy our army a little bit further. If they ride the elephants onto us, we will be trapped."

"No way, master! If we do this, …". He paused for a moment and looked at me in a strange expression.

"Trapped?" and then he burst into laughter.

"You are a genius."

"What?"

"I know how we will overcome the elephants, thanks to you. You inspired me."

"But how?" I understood nothing. He found a genius way out, but what was it?".

"Can you tell me what it is?"

"I will tell you in the headquarters, ok?" Let's go back."

We went back to the headquarters on our horses as fast as possible. Caucasus immediately called all commanders and local leaders for the meeting.

"I have determined the war method that we will follow, and I have formed a new strategy accordingly. Our previous time and defense-based tactics and the orders I have made in this direction are void. Our aim in the war is now to destroy the enemy completely!"

The commanders were puzzled; so was I.

"But we are not many."

"It doesn't matter. The war is won in the headquarters! We are the people who are trying to protect our homeland. If they are invaders, this will help our soldiers to be better motivated and fight better. We are also better in terms of tactics and leadership than they are".

A local leader held the floor: "Your majesty, I have enormous trust in the courage of our soldiers and the talents of yours and our commanders. But what about the elephants? As you know, no battle against elephants has resulted in victory. The only method that works against elephants is to dehydrate them to the desert, but we can't do that because the order is to protect Samara. "

"Don't worry about the elephants. I know what to do."

We were all listening to him holding our breath.

"When I was a child, my father brought me to a fair in the city. There was an elephant at this entertainment where there were men and women with different garments. While the elephant was walking among people, they were feeding and stroking it. While everything was alright, a rat showed up in the fair. Probably it was a rat that got lost or escaped from a cat or even ran for a piece of savory cheese. No one noticed it but the elephant. It was terrifying when it saw the small rat. It began to attack everywhere, flittingly, and escaped. It was so scared and crusty that it turned the fair inside out. Luckily there was no dead, but there were people under crush hazard, and some of them were injured. Now I want to take advantage of it." Addressing to the local leaders, he said: "Tell the people to catch all rats alive in Samara till the war day. Master Tomtom! You and other commanders; increase the production of war guns! I want more production of especially arrow and catapult."

"Catapult?"

"Yes, I want as many catapults as you could produce."

He turned back to the local leaders. "I have heard that this place is famous for its olive oil. Is it true?"

"Yes, sir. We have very qualified olive oil".

"How about your reserves?"

Local leaders thought that he was asking if the reserves would be enough in case of extension of the war.

"Don't worry, sir; we have enough oil for our people and the army at least during a year."

"Great! Then let the preparations begin!"

Then we left the tent. He needed to stay alone to be able to plan and organize any small details or mishaps in the war. So leaving a guard at his door, I strictly ordered him to send the ones who would like to see Caucasus to my tent.

13

Eventually, it was the war day. The enemy forces were before us with their huge army of about seventy divisions. The elephants were equipped with ornaments and shields as well as the army. Besides, there was a very crowded cavalry regiment.

Caucasus had set the army on the way to the headquarters as he had previously determined. We took the steep hills behind us. After the mutual visits of the messengers, both armies took a war position. It was clear that the enemy did not take us seriously despite Caucasus; they knew we were there for distraction.

Our army was more in a corps level. The opponent was formed by the unification of two armies. We still had to do our best. Caucasus hid the archers and the catapults in the hills. Only a catapult and an arrow team were in the center. He did not divide the center into parts; we were all together instead.

The enemy did exactly what we predicted. First, he put his elephants forward. Five hundred elephants with riders and archers on were advancing upon us. An infantry of twenty divisions was following behind. If I didn't know our plan, I would say we are waiting for our suicide until the enemy arrives in the middle of the battlefield.

When our enemies came to the exact place where we wanted them to be, Caucasus gave the order to throw the catapult at the center. Dozens of bags with catapult fell onto the elephants. It was worth seeing the effect of mice coming out of the bags upon elephants. The elephants who had seen the rats started to attack and escape with horror, crushed most of their riders and even caused great damage on the army as they tried to escape to the direction where they came from. This mouse game was so effective that in the future, this war would be called "Battle of the Mice."

Caucasus loved defeating the enemy with clever plans that nobody could think of. He never thought of being so brave or hero as a leader; instead, he had only a result-oriented mind. Although some people were criticizing this feature of him; I think intelligence was the most powerful weapon, and my student was doing the right thing. Today he did the same thing too. He ruled out the enemy's most important trump card with those ordinary rats. The army advancing behind the elephants had lost much being struck with consternation. The army was easily broken in a short time with the help of the archers hidden in the hills as well as the giant rocks of the catapults built up in the same hills. When they completely approached us, our cavalry and five battalions were enough for us to repel the enemy. When the first day ended, and our enemies withdrew to their barracks, the battlefield was heavily covered with their dead soldiers. Both parties had lost half of their troops on the field, but when considered the preponderance, the loss of the alliance's army would not be comparable.

On the second day, there had been a minor collision. Apparently, they wanted to test our strength. Moreover, not being able to know what was on Caucasus' mind worried the enemy commanders. The only noteworthy news was that a Karachi execution team broke into the headquarters at the back of our head and killed a few of our important officers and kidnapped one of them. Unfortunately, we couldn't stop them. I'm sure they had done their well-known torture to our officer, and I think they knew a lot about our power and our plans. Therefore, I even offered to change our plans to Caucasus but he did not accept it. I think he believed in the endurance of the soldiers more than I did.

On the third day, our opponents stated that they wanted to finish the war immediately. Maybe the misdirection of our officer they kidnapped was effective on their decision because if they knew our plan, they would not take the whole army to the battlefield.

Around fifty divisions of the army were on the battlefield. We had a ready position to fight with all of our strength, but we were waiting in a narrow area far beyond the battlefield.

Our enemies attacked with all their forces both to the cavalry and to the infantry. The expected plan of Caucasus was realized fifty yards away to encounter. With my command, hundreds of flammy arrows and kindled catapults are thrown upon the enemy. The genius plan of Caucasus was: Before the enemy came, all the olive oil in the village where the headquarters were established was poured into the battlefield.

Now with all their forces, the enemy was running over the soil covered with olive oil. While the arrows and the rocks we threw killed the enemy soldiers, but the fire trapped the whole army in a big fire. Because the soil absorbed the oil in the last few days, the fire took short, but this was enough for us. The army busy dealing with fire was diminishing with the arrows and catapults of our soldiers second by second.

When the fire stopped, they lost many soldiers in amount, but they were still more than ours. We were lucky because the survivors were scared, shocked, and almost all of them were injured. With Caucasus's sign, we assaulted the rest of this enemy army. They still endured well. The decisive victory was when the sun was about to go down.

14

The royal ambassadors came from the capital before we sent the prisoners. They brought new orders before we could celebrate victory. They wanted us to conquer the Atar Fortress of the Karachis, which couldn't be conquered though it was besieged for two years. We set off unquestioningly, but this matter would be growing longer and longer because the fortress was well-protected and in an inaccessible position. Somehow we couldn't leave it off due to its geographical importance. We tried so hard for it in times of Ayan, but we failed.

When we came to the front of the fortress, Commander Comor, who was charged with the conquest, welcomed us with a ceremony. The rats' victory spread quickly. We spent the first day with celebrations. The Atar people were watching us from the castle with fear and anxiety. Their overconfidence in the power and resistance of their castle was undeniable; on the other hand, Caucasus had the image of the world: "He always wins by hook or by crook. Trust him". That's what disturbs the Atar.

The first saying of Caucasus in the military meeting on the second day was: "Gentlemen, I am not able to stay long because of my busy agenda. We will set off right after the conquest of the fortress."

At first, there was a pause after his speech; then everybody in the meeting burst into laughter even our soldiers next to us gave a smile. There were only two persons who were not laughing; the first one was me and the second one was Comor, who was seriously listening to him. He stood up and said: "Shut up!" taking everybody's attention calling to order. Then, he continued his speech pointing at Caucasus:

"Sir, do you want anything from us to do?"

I appreciated Comor indeed because no one could stand anyone from outside which said "I can handle your two-year-failure within two days," but Comor was a soldier who valued his country's interests above everything. That is what makes a nation strong.

After Caucasus told us what to do, we started to wait for midnight. We had no idea about his plan; all he said was that fifty of the best people were to get ready for midnight. Fifty soldiers came into the woods near the fortress when it was the time. After walking for about ten minutes, a light flashed in the darkness. The Caucasus also shook the torch in his hand in the air and howled like a wolf. At that moment, I noticed two people coming towards us. We, with the weapons on our hands, were on full alert but Caucasus stopped us.

"Welcome, sir!"

"Thanks, guys. Is the tunnel ready?"

"Yes, sir."

"Alright, let's go!"

What tunnel was it?. We didn't understand at all. What was he planning this time? We came to the front of the felled tree. The men we were following began to pick a wide log. Then we noticed a tunnel on the ground.

Comor asked: "What is that?

"A tunnel that goes into the fortress," said Caucasus.

Comor was looking at us puzzled. Everybody was puzzled, indeed. Nobody asked when Caucasus had this tunnel built, why he did not talk about it before or why the siege took long in vain. It was now unimportant. I learned the secret of this tunnel from Caucasus later: Caucasus had the intelligence office build several tunnels and secret passages in the world. Also, he placed his secret men in these crucial points. And these men turned to be loved in that region. They became artisan, farmer, and merchant in time. Even men were working for the state. Ultimately this organization concludes: Caucasus can conquer wherever he desires. He has already placed his men all around the world.

We started to progress in the tunnel we entered. The leading ones had torches in their hands. We stopped after a few hundred yards. One of the men who put us in a tunnel hit the ceiling door cryptically. After a while, the cover was opened. When we went upstairs, we were in an inn. Caucasus had already arranged everything: the men who welcomed us took out clothes in yellow trunks with long black robes and spikes from the crates in the cellar. These were the clothes of Atar's clergy. The Atar was a Karachi fortress and, like all the Karachi people, the Atar people would highly show their respect for the clergy, and since there was a religious meeting tonight, the streets would be full of priests who wore these clothes, which would help us to walk in the streets without attracting any attention.

We wore our clothes and walked out in five or ten-membered groups and started to move on deserted streets. People were either asleep or worshipping in the temple. On the street, there were only military patrols wandering in pairs, and they raised no difficulties. When we arrived at the gate of the fortress, we saw thirty soldiers waiting at the door. The man who opened the door to us went to the castle commander and called on to pray to bless the soldiers all together against the attacks of the barbarians - which are us. Soon after, the soldiers were crouched in front of us with the command of the castle commander. We started mumbling on the sly, and we slowly surrounded them. Before they understood what was going on, we killed off the soldiers with the swords we took out from our robes.

We had very little time before we saw the soldiers passing by. We rushed to the door of the fortress and opened the door, then took out the torches that we kept in our bags, and some of our soldiers started to shake their torches over the castle door. Within a few minutes, thousands of soldiers waiting in the bushes flew out and entered the fortress. Our army was inside now, and the enemy noticed it after all our soldiers had entered. The first morning lights were reverberating over Tonga's flag waving on the tower.

15

One should ask a person who says, "I have experienced everything in life: Have you ever led a triumphant army? Nothing on earth can give someone such a great pleasure. Also we can imagine the contrary scenario. For a commander or for a king, to witness his army defeated or even destroyed is like to witness his entire family killed. We had fallen over backward, and we had never been defeated for a long time thanks to Caucasus. These victories had glorified him on people's eyes. The soldiers loved him so much that they died even with his sign. Not only the soldiers but the entire state and also the people saw him as a myth.

After the conquest of the fortress, the soldiers started to live it up. The commanders also joined this party. I have never seen such an undisciplined army before. If we were attacked at the moment, our state would be devastated. As he said before, Caucasus was ready for his quick return, but the misfortune did not leave us. As soon as we were on our way, the king sent us a new order: He wanted us to conquer a fortress ten days away. But the fortress was in a dangerous place as it was located in the heart of the city. There was a risk of being besieged for us. I couldn't understand exactly why the king asked for this fortress.

After Ulak brought us the news, Caucasus went inside his tent looking up the map. He didn't even notice me enter.

"When will we set off?"

Having his eye on the map, he replied:

"Look at it! What is special with this fortress?"

"Are you questioning the orders?".

"This is the silliest order I have ever received!"

I checked the map, and he was right. It was in the enemy's arms. We needed to occupy at least three more fortresses to be able to capture this fortress safely, which we would have no advantage at all. I shared it with him:

"You are right. This fortress is not special."

Caucasus shook his head:

"No. It is."

I asked him curiously: "What is it?"

"It is too far!" and he stood up and screamed: "I understood my uncle's plan!

"What is his plan?"

"Don't you get it? My uncle's plan is to make me busy around here."

"Why would he do that?"

"I heard last month that my uncle was planning to abdicate and then substitute Aktobe as he was getting old. I learned it later than the king's inner circle. So it was true."

"I didn't know that you have eyes on my uncle's throne."

"No. I just didn't want to start a fight for the throne, but after my uncle abdicates, I have the right". I could walk in the air. I was taken aback, but at the same time, I felt happy.

I blurted out: "Your order my king!"

"Get ready! Off we go!"

"To Kiribati?"

"No, to Saratov!"

16

Saratov was the former capital and the most important city after Kiribati. Also, it was the city of which Aktobe was a governor. Caucasus knew that he could not intervene from the capital, but Saratov was very devoted to him. Although Aktobe had been a governor for years, he didn't have such a strong influence either over the soldier or over the people as Caucasus did. Caucasus intended to enslave Aktobe and to unite the forces in Saratov with the forces in his hands to form a strong army and to defeat the central army of the empire. If he triumphed, this meant that he would be the king. So, not only would he have the son of the king but also would he defeat the king's army. In this case, no one would support Dakar but Caucasus. When considered the extraordinary leadership skills of Caucasus and the powerful army in Saratov, the possibility of success was quite high.

When we arrived in front of the city walls, the fortress door opened. When we entered, the deputy governor greeted us at the door.

"Welcome, dear Caucasus!"

"Where is Aktobe?"

"He is in his palace, your majesty. Let me inform him."

"There is no need. Let's go together."

The Chamberlain never suspected anything. Our army was in. Nobody else knew about our plans. In this case, I could not figure out how the revolution would be. I wished that Caucasus arranged everything.

Caucasus didn't want me to come with him. So I grabbed a snack together with the soldiers, but Caucasus didn't turn back yet after a long time. I was nervous. I had many experiences for years, but I couldn't stop my tension, although I knew what would happen a little later. After a long time, a crowded delegation of Caucasus came along with Aktobe. They came in the middle of the square. Aktobe began to speak; there was a tremor in his voice caused by excitement.

"My valuable soldiers… The control of our city as of today … has temporarily passed to my uncle's son Caucasus. I wish you to respect and show him the same loyalty you did to me".

During the conversation, I noticed a crossbow on the back of Aktobe, and I didn't know when the shooters of Caucasus made it. They placed it on the archer towers without being noticed. That was what made Caucasus great: He never left his job to luck but planned every possibility.

The soldiers and the people of the fortress understood what had happened: a silent, sudden revolution was carried out and there was no grunt except for Aktobe's loyal men. They didn't dare to do anything anyway. The spies of Caucasus had prepared the army ideologically before. So the soldiers were happy indeed, but now everyone in the fortress was more cautious and more stressed because everyone could imagine more or less what they could do next.

Our presumptions came true. Saratov's occupation by Caucasus was shocking in the capital, but what we couldn't predict was that the king was able to prepare such a large army in such a short time. While we were only waiting for the central army, we came across the entire army. Less than a week later, the king sent upon us the main army of the State of Tonga under the command of General Lima. I realized the mistake we made when the Tonga army with 250,000 soldiers appeared on the horizon of Saratov. There was no strategy to be made or a balance of power to create. This war was impossible to be won. Even Caucasus would not succeed. Compared to the crowds of our army, they had advanced technology weapons as well as successful general and officers. Lima was a very good commander too. As a result, Saratov had no chance. The only thing to do was deal.

Some representatives came from the opponents. Caucasus and I met with them at Aktobe's palace. After the long negotiations, we surrendered on condition that no one was punished except us. If Aktobe hadn't been with us, they would have no intention of making a deal. I suppose they would kill off us all. Caucasus! How could you make such a mistake? He had made one mistake in his life, which ruined both him and me.

The youngest son of the king, Iber, came along with the army. In addition to diplomats, there was my former student, Marshall Lima, and the Prince Iber. After the agreement was reached, Aktobe was brought to the room, and our soldiers laid down their arms and surrendered by order of Caucasus.

After he entered the room, Aktobe gave a hug to General Lima with jo, but Lima seemed cold for him.

"Thank you very much, my commander, for saving me. Thank you!" And he gave a hug to his brother. "Thank you, my brother; you have come here to save me. I knew you wrong. I am so sorry."

We couldn't believe in our eyes what was going on at that moment. After hugging his brother, Iber stabbed him at his back with a dagger under his arm. Aktöbe stared at his brother with horror.

We looked at each other, confused with Caucasus. I saw fear for the first time in his eyes, and he did not expect such a betrayal. The diplomats in the room were standing still.

"What did you do?"

Iber replied grinning:

"Me? You're the one who killed my brother!"

"What!". This time I was the one screaming.

Lima cut in:

"Did you see, Caucasus? Playing a game is not your qualification only. Aktobe's death will be over you, so the deal we have made will be out of date, and you will be killed."

Caucasus completed the rest of his speech: "Thus, Iber will be unrivaled."

Iber cut in:

"Exactly my brother!"

I asked my former student: "So what is your interest?"

"To keep my seat, of course. You don't know, do you?".

"Know what?"

"The king has decided to abdicate and substitute Caucasus."

Our both faces turned into white.

Caucasus spoke involuntarily:

"Me?"

"Yeah, your last mission was given to complete the preparations before you arrived. It was only you who could rule this country not only because of your loyalty and success but also because of his injustice to your brother. He didn't trust his two sons. But I couldn't let that happen, because after you became a king, I'd probably be fired. That's why I offered Aktobe to rebel against his father. But …" He looked at me as if he is looking down a corpse on the ground. "Aktobe didn't accept it. He was a fool. I offered it to Iber, he agreed. Together we would have made the revolution and killed the King, but there was no need for it because of your meaningless occupation."

"So…I go to the throne while you and my older brother go to the grave," said Iber.

17

This time we were brought to the city, where we entered victoriously before, as prisoners. This time, we were in a carriage with weak horses, instead of noble horses. The people who read the poems on our behalf, who applauded us in every situation, were now booing us and air their lungs. The girls who were throwing flowers at us every time we went to the city from the Saltanat street were now throwing stones at us. It was one of the most horrible things that could happen to a man on earth: To lose reputation! But I was thinking about Caucasus, not myself; such a great genius should not have faced such an end; it was a great injustice.

What happened just happened.

Tonga's greatest commander was at the end of the road. I looked at his face to see how he was. Again he was like the way before as if he was living in another world. In the meantime, he did not feel the need to protect himself from the pebbles thrown on his face, I wanted to come up to protect him, but it was useless because we were stuck in the prisoner carriage with chains. Despair now covered my whole self. Our fate was inevitable, but I saw a glimmering light in the eyes of Caucasus. He was looking at one point with hope in the crowd. I turned to him to see what he was looking at. I saw someone watching us quietly and sadly, among the people swearing. I knew who it was. This was Mercan who we were accused of killing his future wife.

After being embarrassed and waiting for a few hours, we were brought to the king with our hands in the chain. I never saw the king so sad and collapsed; he had a worn-out look. It hadn't been over a month since I last saw him, but he was like he had aged ten years. I pitied him for the first time. How painful the price of betrayal was!

The king asked only one question after laying eyes on us:

"Why?"

How could he answer it? Because... I deserved the kingdom. Because you betrayed my father. Because ...you took my title of marshall. Because you deserved this! Because no matter how you do wrong to someone, you can't explain to a person why you caused his son to lose. You can't tell the king about the justice of the revolution. We couldn't either wait for the decision about us. King Dakar began to talk after a while:

"I'm not going to hand down a decision on you. My little son Iber, to whom I will hand over my throne and crown tomorrow, is going to decide on your future tomorrow. But when my son decides, I can advise him not to leave justice and compassion. So that's all I can do."

How good! Our lives are in Iber's hand. We would be luckier if they were in an executioner's hand.

When the celebrations for the crown ceremony began, the guards closed us in the dungeon. The dungeon we entered was the Simusir dungeons, which were three times lower than the worst prisoners. The guard put us in two cells side by side and went away. The place where we were closed was too small and dark enough to suffocate those who had claustrophobia. There was no window or light source. When we stood up, our head was touching the ceiling.

I crawled on the ground and hit the door:

"Caucasus! Can you hear me?" I asked. I hit the door again as there was no voice inside. He answered: "Yes, I can hear you, Tomtor."

"Thank you."

"For what?"

"For many beautiful adventures we experienced together."

"I wouldn't want it to end like this."

"It doesn't matter. We contributed a lot to the country, son. The ones who haven't been born yet will understand what we did."

"Maybe we will survive." I smiled.

"My dear student, no one is invincible. Even you. One day it will be over. And it is today."

"Don't we have any chance?"

"I don't know but don't lose your hope anyway."

While we were conversating, we heard the tout's voice coming outside: "Dear people, right after the crown ceremony, we will have the wedding of our new King Iber and the beautiful court girl Mercan Sultan. All our people are invited to the wedding and there is no limit to this ceremony."

After what I heard, I lumped in the throat, how crook Iber was! I wanted to say something, but I stopped. I was uncertain that Caucasus wanted to hear something or not.

18

The moment when everyone was blind drunk at midnight, a girl in a black dress was wandering in front of a derelict house in the woods in the southern part of the city.

It was obvious that she was not very happy. A few soldiers came out of the bushes a little later. They stopped when they saw the girl. Their leader approached the girl: "Will you take us inside?"

She nodded.

"Let's go then. By the way, …"

Showing the hilt of his sword:

"If you trick on us, we will show you our real trick."

The girl was angry instead of being scared. She walked over to the soldier, and the soldier was surprised and stepped back.

"I hope they are not all your stupid threats. If you fail this, I will kill you with my own hands!" she said and showed the dagger she hid in her dress. The man came into the hut without responding. The soldiers followed him.

They barely fit inside.

"You were supposed to get us into the palace. We could have entered this place by ourselves."

The girl didn't answer. She just pushed the stove on the floor aside. Her raising the stove alone and putting the stove aside caused admiration and laughter among the soldiers. There was a large tunnel under the stove that the girl lifted.

"What is this?"

"Don't you want to go to the palace?"

"Yes."

"Then this way." The commander was scared of the darkness of the tunnel and felt angry:

"if this is a trap, you are dead!"

But she did not care about these threats. After igniting one of the pre-prepared torches, she jumped into the hole. Little later, the soldiers did the same.

The soldiers behind and the girl in the front came to the threshold of a stair after walking a lot of paths. They couldn't see the end of the stair. They couldn't go back either. They had to trust her. When they finally reached the top of the stairs, the girl unlocked the door with the key in her pocket.

The girl went in after she said: "Wait a moment." It had been a minute before she came back and opened the door.

"Come in," she said.

The soldiers were stunned by the splendor of the room they entered. It was obvious that this place was inside the palace. The girl gave a map to the commander: "You can go straight to the king's room by following the marked road on this map." The commander snickeringly turned to his soldier: "Go down the path we came from and bring the rest of the army, and we will occupy Tonga tonight! "

19

"You know what? I used to believe that you would plan everything in this life."

"I disappointed you, didn't I?"

"Oh, no! Yes, you are right, indeed. You know we are here."

"I know. We are in the dungeon because of my silly plans."

"Listen, son! You've brought us victory even in the most hopeless times; you've repeatedly saved me and the army from extinction. I'm not going to be arrogant to offend you or to question your genius. Now I understand that everything you did was the acts of a big game. Though it was ridiculous for me at the beginning, the things you did always resulted in our favor in the long run. You were always a kid who knew what you did; you were always one step ahead of us. Everything was under your control, which surprised me. People might lose, make mistakes, but I've always seen you holding control. But now you're incapacitated for the first time. And for the first time, I'm helpless too. I don't see a strategy for the first time. I wish we were in one of your weird games, and we were here for tactics. I wish tonight were nothing but a game".

Right after I finished my words, there was a big noise in the dungeon. Shouting, sword churning, grappling with each other.

"What's going on? or someone swamped in the dungeon?" I was worried, I couldn't understand what was going on, but the Caucasus' voice was still calm as before:

"Here we go, master! This is the last act of the game".

20

The Samoa soldiers were the ones who stormed the dungeon and captured the entire palace within a few hours. I was so surprised. They took us from the dungeon and took us to the palace, and I watched how my Samoa soldiers plundered our capital on the way. But they were plundering everything they saw in the street and all the state buildings. In the meantime, I saw a group of people in front of us. They were the captured Tonga soldiers. There were also the corpses of our soldiers on the streets. I do not know why, but there was no big casualty when compared to the occupation. I thought that the city would not surrender before the entire army was destroyed, which we learned in our military exercises. This occupation was ridiculous and pointless.

When they took us to the king's room in the palace, the person I saw on the throne was the King of Samoa, Shiraz. Yes, I should have accepted it now: Samoa had invaded Tonga, we were now slave, not an independent nation. We were the subjects of another nation. I wish I had died in the dungeon! Oh, I wish I was dead! Our king was standing in front of the throne even though he had two soldiers with him. The poor man was barely standing, no longer as if he was out to live. After a while, a man with a dirty smile, entered and walked to the king, kissed the shoes of the new king. I was ruined once again because that ass-kisser was the Prince Iber, who would become our king. Iberia withdrew back and asked Shiraz for forgiveness for his life. He said if he forgave him, he'd be a slave like until the end of his life, damn it!

Shiraz pointed at him with his hand to be quiet. Then he turned to us. He said: "Obey and live, great warriors!" with great pride. Sucking pig! Did he think that we would be afraid of him and trembled with his majesty? I got so angry that I gathered all my strength and wanted to throw huge saliva onto his hand he extended. But my saliva hit the face of another poor guard. He could not wipe his face because he was at attention. Shiraz was very angry. He jumped up:

"Guards! Take this man…" He was about to give the declaration of my death, but Caucasus stood up:

"Please my king, forgive him. He doesn't know what he said". I was shocked. "What are you doing, Caucasus?". He did more; he kissed Shiraz's hand. I was closing and opening my eyes. I must have been dreaming, which I couldn't wake up from.

Shiraz liked what Caucasus did. He stood up and hugged him.

"Thank you, Caucasus. I couldn't have won this victory without you."

"What?"

A chill ran down not only my back but also Dakar's, the Tonga's and even Iber's. They were all petrified. Shiraz continued:

"If you hadn't let your soldiers into the palace through the secret passage with the help of the spy you sent, we would never have been able to achieve it. Bring her here!" he said.

Mercan entered the room. She was wearing a black dress.

"Honestly, I didn't believe you when I heard from General Dese that you wanted to leave your country to me. But then I realized that you were serious when I learned about your rebelliousness against your uncle and about how you got caught. Of course, I would give you more than your uncle had. I have sent one of my unities under Dese to the zone you told me before though I still have some hesitations." pointing at Mercan: "Your lover took Dese and our soldiers through the tunnel and into the palace.

I remembered General Dese. He was our slave in the war which I didn't attend. Caucasus released him anyway. I didn't believe in what they said. Caucasus can't have been that prick. I smell a rat. Shiraz continued his speech:

"My dear friend, you're my most important ally, the soldiers didn't reciprocate, as we said, we didn't kill them either. I didn't understand how you convinced your troops, but I didn't do any harm to your people, and I didn't make the city fall. You know why? Because I'm an honest man, you kept the promise you made, and I kept mine".

"There was one more promise you made, my king."

"Oh, yes. I announce you the chief commander of both Samoa and Tonga armies of which I am the king."

"Thank you sir."

"Even for your love…" he pointed at me: "I won't keep this insolent alive."

I immediately entreated to Shiraz. "Forgive me, my king, our great savior, when I was out of the dungeon, I lost myself. I will be faithful to you until I die, forgive me!" At that moment I could feel that all Tonga people watching us detested us. So did I. I tricked the king with my flattery. He was calm now.

"When considered what you experienced, you could be treated gently. Ok, I forgive you. You will be the assistant of Caucasus."

He fell into my trap. Oh my gosh! Is he really a king? "Thank you, sir; you will not regret it!"

I knew Caucasus well. He never lowered himself so but he was a professional actor. If he sold the country to Shiraz, he must surely know something. I should also join his drama and see what would happen in the end.

21

There was interesting progress on the day after the occupation. The Karachi were on their way to attack Tonga with all their forces. They learned that Samoa had occupied Tonga, and in this case, Samoa's power was incredibly increasing. The three big states had almost equal military power. This balance had been preserved for centuries by the two states except for short alliances of both countries against the third country, but now it was changing. The two forces united the Samoa and the Tonga, which overturned the balances. It was, of course, unthinkable that the Karachi would remain silent to this progress. That's why Rat -the old emperor Herat's daughter and the new Emperor- gathered a very crowded army and campaigned on us, but the old Shiraz did not care much, so he decided to welcome the army in front of Kiribati. So he could watch the victory and the pleasure of capturing Karachi from the balcony of his new palace. But Caucasus sent the Tonga people to Saratov just in case. Shiraz did not oppose because he already had an intention of clearing the city away from all the Tonga people in the long run. Caucasus was doing whatever Shiraz asked for: sending the people away. It was not difficult to make them never come together.

Shiraz trusted in himself a lot, and he seemed pretty right about what he thought because he had enormous power in his hand: he had both Tonga and Samoa army. Besides, Caucasus, the best commander on earth, was commanding his army. When we had all these things, the victory was inevitable for him.

Anyhow, I think it was a great risk that the war would be near the city walls. They would lose everything if we lost. What of it! I'd better bend down to a teenage girl instead of calling that disgusting man as a king.

It was the day of the war. The red army of Samoa was on our right while Tonga's celestial army was on our right side. On the day before the war, the Karachi army arrived at the plateau where the war would be made and opened its yellow flags and was embattled.

"Won't you still announce it?"

"What?"

"What is the plan?"

"I have already told you in the headquarter!"

"Oh come on! I know you have a trick. I am sure of it because I raised you."

"My only aim is to win the Karachi army and bring peace to the world."

When I burst into laughter, the soldiers around us couldn't stop looking at us.

"You will bring peace to the world, will you? With such a technique? Do you think I believe in this bullshit?"

He shrugged his shoulders unhappily. For a moment, I felt like he was telling the truth, but no way. I took this silly thought out of my mind immediately. I can't imagine such nonsense. As he was Caucasus, he must have a plan.

There was no result after the diplomatic negotiations. The Karachi messenger condemned the occupation and immediately asked the Samoa to release us. How thoughtful people they are! Anyway, the war was about to begin. By the way, the Karachi was able to gather a huge crowded army. But of course, it couldn't be as crowded as ours. This war reminded me of the war in the Tere desert, the same scene.

The enemy, with eight corpses, which meant half of that army, moved forward. Caucasus, on the other hand, sent the entire Samoa army to the battlefield. Our left wing was empty; this was not the style Caucasus was used to. For half an hour the Samoa people and the Karachi went at it hammer and tongs. As the Samoa army was not prepared well and they trusted in us so much, they were almost crushed. I think I understood that his purpose was to have the Samoa army cause to break and take the city back. However, when I was thinking about all these, Caucasus had given orders to all soldiers of the Tonga army to move forward. There were only three divisions left with us. This move broke my dreams, and our army was going to help our invaders. Wait a minute! It wasn't, indeed.

Instead of attacking the Karachi, our army was killing the Samoa.

"Yes!" I cried out.

"I knew it! I knew that you had a plan!"

Caucasus looked at me and smiled. He nodded his head yes but said no words. When I stared at the balcony of the palace, I saw the old and skinny Shiraz stand up in a panic, pulling his long beard and holding his red silk dress. He realized he was deceived. Ayan's son was doing to him what he did to Ayan years ago. There was nothing to do anymore. His entire army was almost destroyed on the battlefield.

The war did not take even two hours, and the entire Samoa army had died with our swords with no slaves. In the meantime, Shiraz was furious about the destruction of his army. Instead of escaping, he closed the city doors tightly. He was going to defend Kiribati. There was nothing else he could do. If he escaped in such a situation, he would not be able to withstand the allied army even if he could reach his country. Kiribati was an almost impossible city to invade.

With its high towers, defensible position and its most advanced defensive vehicles, it is a place which keeps outsiders out.

After the victory, Rat came to us and hugged Caucasus and then kissed him. Luckily Caucasus sent Mercan to Saratov. They celebrated victory together. Rat was a beautiful young girl. With her long hair, blue eyes, and clear white skin, she had all the genetic characteristics of the Karachi. "Darling, it is our victory now." Caucasus smiled and said:

"The victory belongs to the ones who believe it."

"You are a genius. Your plan destroyed the entire Samoa army. We will get married when the Samoa fade from the scene, and we will rule the three countries together."

"Yes, darling but we still have a problem."

"What is it?"

Caucasus pointed at Kiribati:

"Our capital city is still in the enemy's hand."

"Don't worry my love! I will give your city back. It will be our wedding gift for us. My army will be able to enter the city through the secret passages and kill all the Samoa people thanks to the maps you gave me!"

After a while, the Karachi army had entered Kiribati. The Samoa army found themselves among the soldiers who were uncertain where they came from. Caucasus did not build a single tunnel in the city. He let the Karachi in the city as he did for the Samoa people.

The vast majority of the Karachi army was inside, and the city's door opened a little later.

Rat: "Darling, wait for me, I will take the city and bring it to you."

"I'm waiting for you here!" said Caucasus. Rat rode her horse and entered Kiribati together with the rest of the Karachi.

"That is his plan: to destroy the Samoa and unite with the Karachi after getting married to Rat and in this way have three states. Why didn't you tell me about it?"

"I love surprising you. You look tubby oldie when you are surprised". We laughed:

"Well, I got it all, but how about Mercan? She betrayed her country for the sake of you. She risked her life. Will you forget all about them?"

"No, I won't. Besides, Mercan didn't betray her country. She knew about my plans from the beginning."

"Did she?"

"Yes, she did. That's why we fought. She did not want to share my plan. But she was convinced after all I happened to and Iber wanted to have her.

"So you've already calculated all that happened?"

"Yes."

"When?"

"I planned it the night my father was killed. As the years passed, I used every progress to this effect. So I refused to be the king. What I aimed was to end this battle forever."

"How about Rat? She got in the groove with her wedding dress. If you intend to make a harem, both women will kill you. Be careful about them!"

"Rat completed her mission."

"How?"

He raised his hand and punched it in the air, and at that moment dozens of burning arrows were seen in the air, followed immediately by terrible explosions. The arrows were a sign. Caucasus had prepared a unit of death by placing gunpowder all over the city. With the sign, our soldiers inside prepared the mechanism and went out of the secret tunnel just before the explosion. I never saw anything like this before: the whole city was suddenly shattered. It was destroyed with the soldiers who fought in it. Kiribati disappeared. After the explosion, our soldiers entered the city just in case and killed the survivors.

We were the only rulers of the earth, but I still had the burden inside me. Caucasus realized this:

"If you feel sorry for my uncle Dakar, don't worry! I forgive him. I told him about my whole plan yesterday. He will no longer be in politics. Instead, he will spend the rest of his life worshipping, but I ordered my men to strangle Lima last night. He's very dangerous. I forgave Iber despite everything. I gave him the position of his brother in Saratov. He will survive as long as he stays loyal to me. It would be very easy to set up the capital Kiribati again."

"What? I can't believe in you. You are rewarding someone who wants to kill you while you are killing the girl who comes to save you!"

Caucasus frowned down and talked tough:

"I have mercy only for my country".

"Herat killed my father, and I killed his daughter. Here is justice! And Rat's plan was not to marry me after the victory but to get rid of me, which wasn't very difficult for me to learn. I can only get married to a Tonga."

I wasn't set at ease. I said: "But you're a hero for people. What you did is out of place."

He gave a confident smile again and continued: "Think of the common feature of the heroes that history tells us! Is this feature their courage, justice, or mercy? No, not all. All heroes have one thing in common: They have finally triumphed!". I think he was right. Even if brutally, he had only done what he had to do for his own, for his country and the whole world.

22

15 years ago…

I was able to save only Caucasus, the younger son of my friend - the king who died in my arms.

We managed to escape from the enemy's ambush with my men. When we were discussing about what we would do with the commanders Dakar's messenger arrived. Dakar ordered us to return to Kiribati immediately. The Prince guaranteed the lives of Caucasus and ours. Normally, I wouldn't believe in such a guy but there was nothing to do. There was no place to escape or hide either. Tonight we were enemies of all.

We finally decided. We would return to the capital with the rest of the troops and Prince Caucasus and pledged loyalty to Dakar, but the only requirement was the life of Caucasus. If he tried to touch Caucasus, all the generals would revolt. Burke said it to the messenger himself. If they touched Caucasus, the whole army would revolt against Dakar. The messenger gulped and said he would forward it. He had his eyes on Burke's huge sword.

I went out of my tent to another tent where I placed Caucasus. I wanted to check him. When I went inside, Caucasus and his friend Mercan were sitting on a stool. Caucasus was writing something vehemently. Mercan was watching him with excitement. Caucasus was ten years old while Mercan was only five years old; she was absolutely in love with him. She never used to sleep before he slept.

"Prince Caucasus, why are you still awake? We will set off early in the morning; please go and get some sleep. As you are awake, Mercan doesn't want to sleep."

Caucasus said nothing. Mercan turned to me and put her little finger on her mouth:

"Shhhh! Uncle Tomtor, we are making a revenge plan." She said it so cute that I burst into laughter. On the other hand, Caucasus kept pretending as if I wasn't there.

The paper rolls that Caucasus had filled with writings and pictures were on the floor. I got them in my hand.

There were: Secret men... the formula of gunpowder... change the direction of the river... exploding ships... enter the dungeon delude the blue... delude the red... delude the yellow... Detonate Kiribati... catapults... archer regiments... tunnels everywhere...invade Saratov...

Such illogical writings on the paper... I couldn't understand anything, but I had to respect the imagination of a child who lost his father.

Anyway, I got the papers in his hand and put him to sleep. When Caucasus went to bed, Mercan did the same. She was still looking at Caucasus, waiting for him to get up.

I put them both to sleep and gave a kiss on their forehead.

When I was about to leave, Mercan called me: "Uncle Tomtor, did you know that I was the first of the secret men? Caucasus counted me in the Secret Men team."

I smiled: "How lucky you are. I wish he could count me in too."

"Let's ask him. Caucasus, shall we count uncle Tomtor in the team?"

He was so cute that I couldn't keep myself laughing. However, Caucasus was looking serious.

"No, Mercan. Uncle Tomtor has a different mission." To be honest, it was weird for me to see Caucasus serious. I thought that it was just the imagination of a child. I clothed him.

"Good night, my prince and my daughter," said I. They had already fallen asleep before I left the tent. I was still looking at the papers Caucasus drew. They were casual pictures like falling rocks, exploiting cities, men shooting arrows.

I properly placed the papers on the stool. At that night, I wouldn't fancy that these drawings and writings, which I thought as a child's imagination, would turn into strategies that would change the fate of all humanity.

-THE END-

www.ingramcontent.com/pod-product-compliance
Lightning Source LLC
Chambersburg PA
CBHW070807120626
46557CB00002B/742